THE EXTRAORDINARY FILES

Atlanta

Paul Blum

RISING★STARS

'The Truth is inside us.
It is the only place where it can hide.'

nasen
Helping Everyone Achieve
nasen

NASEN House, 4/5 Amber Business Village, Amber Close,
Amington, Tamworth, Staffordshire B77 4RP

Rising Stars UK Ltd.
22 Grafton Street, London W1S 4EX
www.risingstars-uk.com

Text © Rising Stars UK Ltd.
The right of Paul Blum to be identified as the author of this work has
been asserted by him in accordance with the Copyright, Design and
Patents Act 1988.

Published 2007
Reprinted 2008

Cover design: Button plc
Illustrator: Aleksandar Sotiroski
Text design and typesetting: pentacor**big**
Publisher: Gill Budgell
Project management and editorial: Lesley Densham
Editor: Maoliosa Kelly
Editorial consultant: Lorraine Petersen

British Library Cataloguing in Publication Data.
A CIP record for this book is available from the British Library.

ISBN: 978 1 84680 179 2

Printed by Craft Print International Limited, Singapore

CHAPTER ONE

June 2006 Bodmin Moor.

Farmer Robson got out of his tractor. He was blinded by a bright light. He looked up into the sky and saw a star-shaped object shooting by. It roared like a lion. He put his hands over his ears.

He ran into the house and phoned the police.
That night all the phone lines were busy. The police
got over 100 calls about a star-shaped UFO.
The police gave the strange plane a nickname.
They called it 'Atlanta'.

London Vauxhall
M15 Headquarters.

Turnbull went to see her boss, Commander Watson.

"Sit down, Laura," he said.

"Sir, I am worried about Parker," she said. "He is working too hard."

"Isn't working hard what we pay you for?" he laughed.

"But he can't *stop* working. He is working on the Atlanta case day and night," she said. "I am doing all our other work."

"How is he doing on the Atlanta case?"
the commander asked.

"Parker says he is about to make a big breakthrough,"
she replied.

Commander Watson looked strangely worried.

"What sort of breakthrough?" he asked.

"Parker didn't say," she replied.

The commander went to the window. He looked out over the River Thames. "So what do you want from me?" he asked.

"Could you let Parker and me have two weeks on the Atlanta case? Give our other work to another team of detectives?"

The commander was silent. Then he said, "I can do something much more useful. I can make Parker take sick leave for one month."

"But Sir ..."

"What you have told me gives me no choice. Parker is mentally exhausted."

"He will never agree to that," she said.

"He will do as he is told," snapped the commander, "or I will have him pensioned off because of ill health."

Turnbull was upset. She had wanted to help Parker but everything had gone wrong. She went to tell him what the commander had said.

"Sent on sick leave," he shouted. "Don't talk rubbish, Turnbull."

"Turn that silly computer off while I am talking to you," she said.

"I am too busy," he said.

"Well you aren't busy now!" She pulled the plug out.

"Are you mad?" he shouted. "I might lose important information about the Atlanta case!"

"And you might lose your partner if you go on like this," she replied. "You are being sent on sick leave *because* of the Atlanta case."

"What does that mean?" he asked.

"They think you are working too hard."

"That is not the real reason. I think I know why they are sending me home."

"Yes?" she asked.

"I am getting too close to the truth."

"But that is our job," Turnbull replied.

"Not if the truth will upset the Secret Service."

"Look Parker. Go home. You are upsetting me."

"You are just the same as the rest of them. You don't want to know the truth if it puts your job in danger."

"That's not fair," she replied.

"So why am I just an agent and you are the captain? Think about it Turnbull."

He went out and banged the door.

CHAPTER TWO

Turnbull was very upset. She had never had a row with her partner like this one. Maybe he is right about me, she thought.

Turnbull turned on the computer. She began to look at the details of the Atlanta case carefully. What was Parker on about? She was his boss, she should know.

Three hours later she was still working when the phone rang.

"Turnbull, it's me, Parker."

"Agent Parker, I am glad to hear from you."

He was silent for a moment and then he said, "I'm sorry about what I said. It was out of order."

"And I'm sorry for not listening to you," she replied.

"I want you to do something for me," he said.

"Do you want to see Overlord?" she asked.

"How do you know about Overlord?" he said.

"I know how your mind works, Parker. And I have been reading your e-mails. So who is Overlord and what does he know about the Atlanta?"

"I don't know."

"Then I suggest, Agent Parker, that we see him together."

They went to Bodmin Moor. When they arrived Parker looked at a map and checked his compass.

"This is our meeting point," he said.

Turnbull peered out of the window. "You could have fooled me. This is the middle of nowhere. Are you sure you've got that map the right way up?"

Then they saw a strange figure walking towards them.
They went to meet him.

"Don't come any nearer," Overlord said.

"What do you want to tell me about the Atlanta?"
Parker asked.

"Who is the woman?" Overlord demanded.

"Agent Turnbull — my partner."

Overlord pointed to the sky. "What you will see here
is the future."

He walked into the darkness without another word.

They waited for twenty minutes. Nothing happened.

"This isn't exactly exciting," Turnbull said, looking at her watch. "If this is the 'future' — give me the 'present' anytime."

Suddenly they were blinded by a bright light. A huge spaceship hovered in the sky. It threw a laser light onto a field. Then it disappeared.

"Incredible," said Parker, rubbing his eyes.

"It was even more exciting than the X files,"
Turnbull said.

They went to the field. They found a dead sheep.
Parker shone his torch onto it.

"Incredible. There is not even a burn mark," he said.

"So what killed it?" Turnbull asked.

"We will find that out back in the lab," he replied. "I'll go and get the car."

"What for?" she asked. "We can walk back to it."

"Not with a dead sheep," Parker said.

"What are you on about?"

"I can't call up forensic to take the sheep away. I am on sick leave, remember."

Parker started to pull the body of the dead sheep.

"And you want me to help you to do that?" Turnbull moaned. Parker nodded.

"You owe me one great big favour for tonight," she replied. "Don't let anyone say I don't roll my sleeves up for my partner."

CHAPTER THREE

They were back at the lab. Turnbull let Parker in through the back door. They dragged the sheep in.

Parker worked quickly. He got very excited. Turnbull chatted.

"This is fantastic!" he said.

"It looks like a dog's dinner. I can see why I gave up eating meat," she replied.

"The vital organs are not damaged," he muttered.

"How did you get to be a surgeon, Parker?" she asked.

"How did you get to be a karate black belt?" he replied.

"I guess it takes all types in this job," she said.

He put some slides under a microscope. "Come and look at this."

"Do I have to?" Turnbull got up and peered through the lens.

"Look at the cells. They have changed shape. They have no DNA in them. The sheep has had all its genes stolen!"

"So she has nothing to wear," Turnbull joked.

Parker was too busy to hear her.

"No wonder the agency wanted to keep this a secret!" said Parker. "They must be very frightened. An alien life force that can kill without leaving a mark. An alien life force that can take the secrets of life as we know them."

Turnbull yawned. "I need some sleep. I think you should go home before the commander finds out you are here and puts us both on sick leave."

The next morning Agent Turnbull went to see Commander Watson again.

"Sir, I am still worried about the Atlanta case," she said.

"Why is that Agent Turnbull?" he replied.

"I have looked into it since Parker was sent home."

"And?"

"And I think I saw the Atlanta the other night."

"You what?" he shouted, rising from his seat.

"A large spaceship. It was very fast. Very bright."

"Look Turnbull, how can I say this? Don't ask questions about the Atlanta."

"But asking questions is my job, Commander."

"Turnbull, the Atlanta is a secret," he whispered. "It's a very expensive spy plane. Built by the Americans. The less you know the better."

"But, Sir, it is my case. I am a detective in the Secret Service."

"Listen carefully, Laura. You have a great career ahead of you. Don't destroy it by asking too many questions."

She was silent. She was shocked. The commander laughed nervously.

"Go away and work on your other cases. There must be lots to do."

"And Agent Parker?" she asked.

"I will sort him out. He just needs a holiday. Maybe you both do."

Turnbull went to Parker's flat. She was angry and upset. Parker comforted her. "Why are you so surprised, Turnbull?" he asked.

"I thought we were all working on the same side."

"Well sometimes we are," he said, "and sometimes we're not. You can't always trust Commander Watson."

"He is talking about us both taking a holiday," she said.

"So we haven't much time. Overlord has asked to see us again. We must leave at once!"

27

They went to Bodmin Moor again. Overlord came out of nowhere towards their car. Turnbull tried to look at his face but he hid it from her again. "Follow me," said Overlord.

They followed him through the long grass. Suddenly they saw the Atlanta. It had landed in a field.

The whole area was lit by a bright light.

"Wow," said Turnbull.

"Incredible," said Parker.

Overlord took them close to the big ship. They had to cover their eyes from the bright light.

"You have been chosen to see great things," he told them. "I can show you but I cannot make you understand".

Suddenly a blue light hit them. They thought of the dead sheep and threw themselves to the ground. They fell into a deep sleep and had a dream. In the dream they saw Overlord take off his hood and they saw that he had no face. Then they saw many spaceships like the Atlanta landing on the River Thames. The people of London were running towards the spaceships but it was hard to see if they were happy or sad.

The two agents woke up. Overlord and the Atlanta had gone. They talked about the dream.

"What does it mean?" asked Turnbull.

"I don't know," said Parker. "Maybe it is the future."

"We must go and tell Commander Watson what we have seen," she said.

"We must do no such thing!" he said. "He will put us on sick leave for the rest of our lives."

"But it is our duty," she said.

"Sometimes it is our duty to say and do nothing."

"Parker, what do you mean?"

"The Secret Service is not ready for news like this. Now is not the time. What did they say the Atlanta was?"

"A spy plane," she said.

"And was it?"

"No."

"They were lying to you and now you want to tell them more?"

"Parker, it is my duty to tell my boss about this. We cannot break the rules."

She ran off into the darkness. He found her by the car.
He handed her the keys.

"You drive back. Say what you have to say.
Commander Watson can pick me up here," he said.

She opened the car door. Then she stopped.

"Go on Agent Turnbull. Tell them what you saw.
Do your duty."

She turned round. She gave the car keys back to him.

"Don't be silly, Parker. I trust you." She took his hand.
"And anyway I don't want to drive round in circles on
this moor all night. I need you and your compass."

He smiled at her little joke and they drove off.

London Vauxhall M15 Headquarters

Two weeks later Turnbull visited Commander Watson for a third time.

"You again," he said.

"Sorry, Sir. I have a favour to ask."

"What sort of favour, Turnbull?"

"It's Parker, Sir. He is feeling much better."

"How can you tell, Agent Turnbull?"

"He has stopped talking about the Atlanta case. He wants to get back to work on the other cases."

The commander smiled. "Parker is one of my best men. I am glad he has come to his senses."

"He has, Sir."

"Well, we must get him back. Just let me make a few phone calls to my boss."

Commander Watson took Turnbull out to lunch. She went so that she could stay in his good books.

While they were out, three men broke into Parker's office. They took away everything to do with the Atlanta case. They smashed Parker's computer and burnt his papers. Nothing of the Atlanta case was left.

CHAPTER FOUR

Turnbull and Parker were in the middle of Bodmin Moor at night again. Parker was showing Turnbull how to use his compass. "Didn't they teach you this in the secret agent classes?" he said.

"Didn't they teach you basic self-defence and combat skills?" she snapped.

"Yeah, but I didn't like all the rough stuff," he said.

They stood waiting for something to happen.
"Are you sure this is the right place?" she asked.

"Yes. This is the place where we met them before."

They waited for one hour but there was
no sign of Overlord or the Atlanta.

"What will we do?" she said.

"We will come back on the anniversary of
my first meeting with Overlord. We must
hope they come back again," he said.

"And what about all the things we saw?"

"We must remember them. But we must
not write them down," he said.

"But I will forget," she replied. "That is
why I have some notes in this book."

"Give it to me, please," he demanded.

He read some pages of it with his torch.
"Agent Turnbull — do you trust me?"
he asked.

"You know I do."

"Really trust me."

"Yes."

"Turn round and close your eyes."

She did as he asked. Parker dug a hole and put the
notebook in it. He set it alight. She turned round.

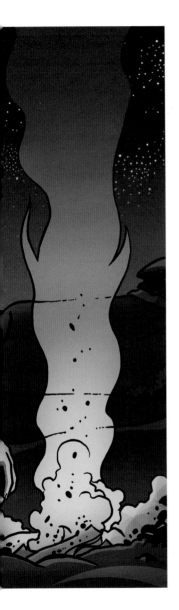

"Parker, what are you doing?"

"I had to destroy it."

"But I will need it — in the future."

"Do you think that the people who destroyed all my records on the Atlanta case will leave you alone? If they found that book what would they do to you?"

"But Parker ..."

"Trust me."

"So how do we remember it?"

"In our heads," he replied.

"But ..."

"Laura, you like watching the 'X Files' on TV, don't you?" he said.

"Yes."

"Laura, the real X Files are so secret that a record is never kept of them."

"The real X Files?" she asked.

"The real X Files are the truth. The truth is extraordinary. The truth is inside us. It is the only place where it is safe," Parker said seriously.

They drove back to London in silence.

GLOSSARY OF TERMS

breakthrough discovery of some important information

come to his senses to stop having silly ideas

compass an instrument for finding your way

detective a person who investigates crimes

DNA deoxyribonucleic acid, the code of life

dog's dinner a mess

favour a good deed

forensic a department which collects scientific evidence for legal use

genes things in a body which determine physical characteristics

hovered floating in the air

M15 government department responsible for national security

nickname a made-up name for someone

out of order wrong

pensioned off early retirement

roll up my sleeves for to work hard for

sick leave time off work because of illness

UFO Unidentified flying object (eg a flying saucer)

QUIZ

1 What is the Atlanta?

2 Where did the Atlanta land?

3 What is a UFO?

4 What is the name of Agent Turnbull's boss?

5 Who do Agents Turnbull and Parker meet on Bodmin Moor?

6 What killed the sheep?

7 What did Agents Turnbull and Parker dream about?

8 Why was Parker's office broken into?

9 What did Parker do with Turnbull's notebook?

10 What do the real X files contain?

ABOUT THE AUTHOR

Paul Blum has taught for over twenty years in London inner-city schools.

I wrote The Extraordinary Files for my pupils so they've been tested by some fierce critics (you!). That's why I know you'll enjoy reading them.

I've made the stories edgy in terms of character and content and I've written them using the kind of fast-paced dialogue you'll recognise from television soaps. I hope you'll find The Extraordinary Files an interesting and easy-to-read collection of stories.

ANSWERS TO QUIZ

1   An alien spaceship

2   On Bodmin Moor

3   An unidentified flying object

4   Commander Watson

5   Overlord

6   A beam of light from the Atlanta. It stole all the DNA from the sheep

7   Spaceships invading London

8   Parker knew too much and the authorities wanted to destroy the evidence

9   He burnt it

10 The truth